S0-BCX-434

Imagination is
a wonderful place to visit!

A FLIGHT OF MARCEAU

Water For All

BY
JOE BROWN

PAINTINGS BY STEPHEN MARCHESI

3/15

MAJESTIC EAGLE PUBLISHING CO.
CHICAGO, ILLINOIS

To my beautiful family —
All 24 of us.
(How lucky am I?)

Published by
Majestic Eagle Publishing Co.
6649 Navajo
Lincolnwood, IL 60712

Copyright © 2013 by Joe Brown
All rights reserved.

No part of this book may be used or reproduced in any manner whatsoever without written permission,
except in the case of brief quotations embodied in critical articles and reviews.
For information contact Majestic Eagle Publishing Co. (jola1@aol.com)
TheFlightsofMarceau.com

First Edition
Printed in USA

Library of Congress Cataloging in Publication Data
Joe Brown, 1935–
Water For All–A Flight of Marceau

ISBN 978-0-9797495-6-8

DESIGNED BY MARY KORNBLUM, CMYK DESIGN INC.
PRODUCED BY DELLA R. MANCUSO, MANCUSO ASSOCIATES INC.

Marceau is my name and this is my tale
I've traveled the seas on the back of a whale
I've flown the sky on a great eagle's wings
And done many other incredible things. . .   Incredible = wonderful

I just heard a story that was really exciting
About animals and Marceau and a whole lot of fighting.
Marceau had to leave, he had something to do
But he said it was ok if I told it to you.
So sit back, my young friend, try closing your eyes
Your imagination is in for an exciting surprise.

While Marceau was on safari in Africa, he saw
An incredible panorama that filled him with awe...

Safari = trip to a jungle
Panorama = wide view
Awe = wonder

Use your imagination—
Can you picture the scene?
If you can, then just do it and you'll know what I mean!

Imagine a waterfall, three hundred feet high
That pours like a river from high in the sky.   Pours = flows
With colors like violet and lilac and white
This waterfall is an incredibly beautiful sight.
As water cascades, white mist takes its place   Cascades = pours
While rainbows dance softly all over the place.   Mist = light rain

At the foot of the waterfall stands a peaceful lagoon   Lagoon = shallow lake
Where animals would gather in late afternoon.   Gather = get together
They come every year when the season turns dry
For the life-giving water the falls would supply.

Had you been on that African safari with me
What kind of animals do you think you might see?
Well, you'd see buffalo and gazelles and antelopes galore   Galore = many

Leopards and lions and so many more,
Beautiful birds dressed in scarlets and blues,
Thousands of zebras and a whole lot of gnus.

Apes and baboons, elephants too,
More than you ever could see in a zoo.
Some of the things are simply preposterous
Like the birds who eat lunch atop a rhinoceros!

Scarlet = bright red
Gnu = wildebeest, silent G,
rhymes with to

Preposterous = silly
Atop = upon

Or you may have seen a tiger or two, maybe three,
Or a dik dik, or hyena, had you been there with me.　　Dik dik = tiny antelope
But since you were not, I'll just tell you about it –
I'm certain this happened; there's no reason to doubt it.　　Doubt = don't believe

They gathered at the lagoon as we all knew they would
And got along with each other, since each understood
That the water was vital, they had learned to expect it,   Vital = necessary
Every animal has rights and each must respect it.

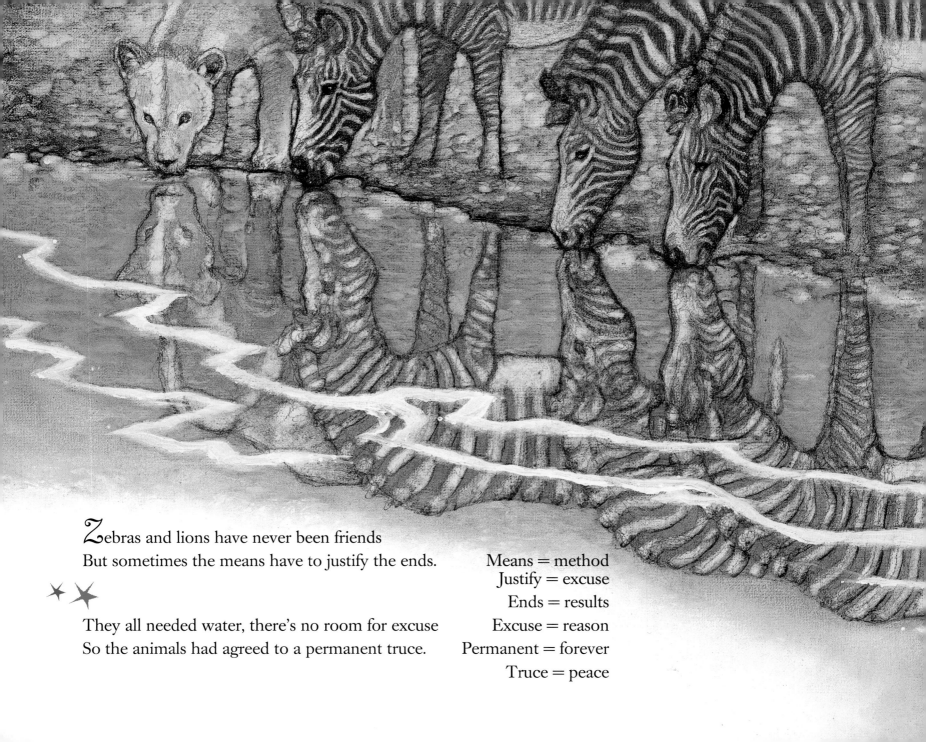

Zebras and lions have never been friends
But sometimes the means have to justify the ends.

They all needed water, there's no room for excuse
So the animals had agreed to a permanent truce.

Means = method
Justify = excuse
Ends = results
Excuse = reason
Permanent = forever
Truce = peace

Each drank from the lagoon with a stranger beside
As they've done since forever, with no need to hide.
"Hello," said the lion who greeted the gnu
The gnu said, "I'm fine, and good morning to you."
They drank of the water, so fresh and so cold
With the beauty around them, a sight to behold.   Behold = witness

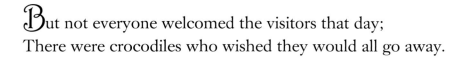

But not everyone welcomed the visitors that day;
There were crocodiles who wished they would all go away.

The meanest of all, the boss of the float   Float = group of crocs
Was a reptile named Crafty, who was big as a boat.   Reptile = lizard-like
"We live here," he bellowed, "all day and all year   Bellowed = yelled
None of those animals even live around here."

"If they all drink our water, we won't have enough. . .
It's time for us crocs to start getting tough."   Tough = strong

So the crocodiles decided that today was the day
When finally and forever they would scare them away.
Slowly and silently they swam in formation.   Formation = pattern
Crafty and the crocs quivered with anticipation.   Quivered = shook
                                                           Anticipation = hope

The animals froze when the reptiles came near;
The movement of crocodiles filled them with fear.
The crocodiles threatened; they started to shout,
"Leave now, everybody, or you'll never get out."

Crocs thrashing and slashing and dashing and splashing
And smashing and flashing and bashing
and crashing!

Every animal was frightened clear out of the lake
To be messing with crocodiles is a gigantic mistake!   Gigantic = really big
You can't stop a croc – they're too fast, they're too strong,
Whoever tries to fight them won't last very long.

The animals could no longer drink, the danger was high
How lucky that Majesty and Marceau had been just passing by.
They had come to see the waterfall and its mystical glow
When they were interrupted by a disturbance directly below.

★★

Marceau seems to appear where ever he's needed

★ Please help us!
we heard, as the animals pleaded.

Interrupted = stopped
Disturbance = noise

Pleaded = begged

Things were not going as the animals had planned
So they got our attention and asked us to land.
We landed, had a meeting and agreed on a plan
And in less than a minute our efforts began. . .
A crocodile in the water is a problem, indeed.
We must make them come out if we hope to succeed.

Did you know that an elephant herd awaits his command?
Well, Marceau called on his friends: would they lend us a hand?
He had saved a baby elephant and to her family he gave her,
So his friend Toby, her father, still owed him a favor.

Marceau called, "Toby, its me, I need you, my friend."
He heard me and answered, as he came 'round the bend.
He said, "Marceau, you look well, perhaps a bit older"   Perhaps = maybe
As he slid his trunk tenderly over my shoulder.   Bit = little

"It would be our pleasure to help you, so just tell me how
And I'll gather every bull, every calf, every cow."

He listened to the plan, very anxious to start;
I could depend upon Toby to handle his part.

Bull = male elephant
Calf = baby elephant
Cow = female elephant
Anxious = eager
Depend = rely

But even elephants may not be enough;
Crocs are mean critters, and these guys are tough.   Critter = living thing
We needed some muscle and we needed some speed
Hippopotamuses are the answer – that's what we need!

When I found them, the hippos were all busy eating.
They were attending their annual family club meeting.   Annual = yearly
Helga Hippopotamus said she'd be pleased to assist
Her relatives came also, they just couldn't resist.

It got very, very scary
when the crocs came on land,
There was snapping and thrashing and nowhere to stand.
As they crawled further ashore the animals ran
But, believe it or not, that was part of our plan.
As the animals backed slowly away from the shore
The crocodiles followed to scare them some more.

As the reptiles crept closer, the animals drew back,
Now our trap had been set – it was time to attack
Because now on the shore, only crocodiles stood.
This was the time to get rid of them, if ever we could.

When Toby heard my signal for the herd to attack
The elephants stampeded, they held nothing back.
They kicked and chased crocodiles, that turned out to be fun,
And the whole gang of reptiles was now on the run.

Reptile = crocodile, etc.
Crept = moved quietly

Stampeded = charged

But then Ellie, the baby, chased a croc in the water
And the herd had to follow to save Toby's daughter.

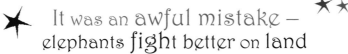

It was an awful mistake –
elephants fight better on land

So now the crocs, once again, had the cold, upper hand.
An elephant moves slowly in water, like a big, heavy raft
And swimming freely among them, the crocodiles laughed.
"Come on, you fat elephants, now you're in trouble
We will bite you on the belly and you'll burst like a bubble!"

The crocodiles attacked, their jaws started snapping
But they had not paid attention and we caught them all napping.
They were totally unprepared for the rest of our plan –
Maybe elephants can't swim fast, but hippopotamuses can. . .

Marceau called for the hippos, as previously arranged,
And it didn't take long for the advantage to change

For the hippos came crashing from out of the brush
And charged at the crocs in a wild, frenzied rush.
Hippopotamuses are huge, about as big as your van
If anything can scare crocodiles, a hippo sure can!
Crash, bam, bada boom, were the only sounds heard.
The crocs stopped cold when they saw what occurred.

When the crocodiles panicked we all got our wish
Because a hippo, in the water, can swim like a fish.
So when the hippos hit the water, the crocs turned around
And they left in a hurry without making a sound.

Previously = earlier
Arranged = set up
Advantage = edge
Brush = bushes
Frenzied = excited

Panicked = got scared

"Uh-oh," said Crafty, "our day has been spoiled.
Run for your lives, boys, our plot has been foiled!"
They slithered away, feeling quite ill at ease,
The invasion of hippos made them weak in the knees.
Now the crocs are afraid if they ever came back
The hippos and elephants would renew their attack.

Plot = plan
Foiled = stopped
Ill at ease = worried
Invasion = attack

Renew = do it again

Now the lagoon is very safe, a safe place indeed
And the animals can take whatever they need.
Today, in the heat of the sun or the cool of the moon
Happiness has returned to the peaceful lagoon,
And as long as the waterfall continues to nourish
The animals of the jungle will continue to flourish.

Indeed = for sure!

Continues = doesn't stop

Nourish = feed

Flourish = grow

We're at the end of the tale and that's all I can say
But remember, tomorrow is just one day away
You'll hear another great story if nothing delays you. . .
Wait!
It's more than just great,
it will surely amaze you!

About the author

JOE BROWN lives in the village of Lincolnwood, Illinois, with his wife, Lola. He was an attorney in Chicago for fifty years until he received a gift of a writing career for his 70th birthday. Bop, as he is known in the family, started writing these stories for his children in the 1960s. After retiring he began, again, writing about Marceau's adventures. He has been reading these stories in schools all over America.

Imagine A Waterfall is his seventh children's book.

About the artist

STEPHEN MARCHESI has illustrated numerous picture books, textbooks and magazines. A graduate of Pratt Institute, his books have been on the Children's Book Council bestsellers list and on the Bank Street College Children's Book of the Year lists. He lives with his wife and son in Croton-on-Hudson, New York.

Imagination is
a wonderful place to visit!